This book is dedicated to my
family for always supporting me
throughout all my endeavors.

*Successville*
Copyright © 2019 by Noah Harris

*Illustrations by Andrew Thomas*

Publisher's Cataloging-in-Publication data
Harris, Noah.
Successville : Noah Harris.
ISBN 978-0-578-42504-7

Mrs. Jones is a teacher who loves
when her students learn.

She wants all the kids in her class
to have a bright future.

Today, Mrs. Jones is trying to teach her second-grade class a math lesson, but no one is paying attention.

"Again? How will my class learn if they never listen?" she sadly asks herself.

"How are my students ever going to succeed in life?"

Mrs. Jones knows she has to think of something to get her class back on track.

After some thought, she has an idea! Tomorrow will be different.

"Boys and girls, today I want to tell you about a place called Successville," says Mrs. Jones with great excitement.

"Everyone has a Successville, and everyone's is a different place. Kate, yours is different from mine, and Austin, yours is different from Peyton's."

The kids are hooked. They all want to make it to Successville. "Mrs. Jones, how do we get there?" asks Will. "I want to go."
"Yea me too," Maria adds.

"Develop talents, set your goals high, work hard, and you will make it there one day!" Mrs. Jones replies. "Never forget honesty is the best policy, and always treat others the way you want to be treated!" she adds.

Austin rushes home after an exciting day at school. "Mom, Mrs. Jones told us about this place called Successville," he shouts eagerly. "Can I go someday?"

"Sure you can, but only if you are willing to work hard," she replies. "You will have to do much better in school, and no son of mine is going to Successville without a talent."

"Hard work, goals, and talents?" Austin asks himself. Getting to Successville is harder than he thought.

Kate tosses and turns all night thinking about what Mrs. Jones said. Kate knows she will have to work a lot harder to be successful.

"Hard work, goals, talents, hard work, goals, talents," she thinks nervously. "Must...Get...To...Successville."

At recess the next day, the kids have a special meeting.

"I can't stop thinking about this Successville place," Maria says.

"Me neither, I want to go so badly," Will replies.

"If we want to make it to Successville, we are going to have to step up our game. I'm in if you guys are," urges Peyton.
"Yea! let's do it," they all agree.

From that point on, the kids are determined to go to Successville. They pay attention in class. They get good grades. They even join clubs to help others. Mrs. Jones is thrilled!

Austin works hard to study for school.
He aces all his classes.

Kate practices her talents. She takes up music and swims every day to become the best.

Peyton dreams bigger than ever before. She sets goals to make her dreams come true.

Years pass, and they are well on their way.
For now, it is time to celebrate. Graduation is
the first stop on the long road to Successville.

Peyton reached for the stars until she could touch them. She became an astronaut. Her Successville is in space.

Austin's Successville is in the White House.
He worked harder than he thought possible
and became President.

Kate swam herself into the record books at the Olympic Games with a gold medal. The Olympics is her Successville.

Everyone has a Successville.
They are all great places, but you have to be
willing to work hard, set goals, and develop
talents. When you do those things,
you will be on your way too!

# SUCCESSVILLE

Where is your Successville?

_____

Made in the USA
Columbia, SC
01 December 2020